To Melissa
D.K.

For my mum, with much love
R.B.

This edition published by Parragon in 2012
Parragon
Chartist House
15–17 Trim Street
Bath BA1 1HA, UK
www.parragon.com

Published by arrangement with Meadowside Children's Books
185 Fleet Street, London, EC4A 2HS

Text © Diana Kimpton 2006
Illustrations © Rosalind Beardshaw 2006

Printed in China

The Lamb-a-roo

Diana Kimpton

illustrated by
Rosalind Beardshaw

PaRragon

Bath · New York · Singapore · Hong Kong · Cologne · Delhi
Melbourne · Amsterdam · Johannesburg · Shenzhen

In the middle of the wilderness was a lamb.
He was very small, very sad and all alone.
"*Maa*," said the lamb. "I want a *maa*."

Not far from the middle of the wilderness was a kangaroo. She had
lots of friends, plenty of relatives and as much food as she wanted
to eat. But she wasn't happy. She didn't have a baby. The kangaroo
felt very sad. One day, she hopped away from her friends
and relatives. She hopped all the way to the middle
of the wilderness and there she found . . .

the lamb!
"*Maa, Maa,*" said the lamb.
The kangaroo loved him right away.

She popped him in her pouch and hopped back to
show everyone her wonderful new baby. The lamb felt safe in her
pouch. He wasn't alone anymore and he was happy. He loved
his new maa and all his new friends and relatives.

Only one thing worried him.

He was different
from everyone else.

Everyone else in
the family had smooth
brown fur but he was
covered with thick,
white wool.

Everyone else in
the family could do
huge jumps, but he
could only do
little ones.

The lamb practiced his jumping every day.

He jumped on his front feet.

He jumped on his back feet.

He jumped on all four feet together. But he couldn't jump higher at all.

Maybe it's because my back legs are too short,
thought the lamb, so he tried to make them grow.

He pulled them. He pushed them.

He even tried to stretch them. But they didn't get bigger at all.

Then one day, not far from the middle of the wilderness, the lamb and his new family found an old house. It was empty. All the people had gone away and no one lived there anymore.

The lamb went exploring.
Beside the house, he found a shed.

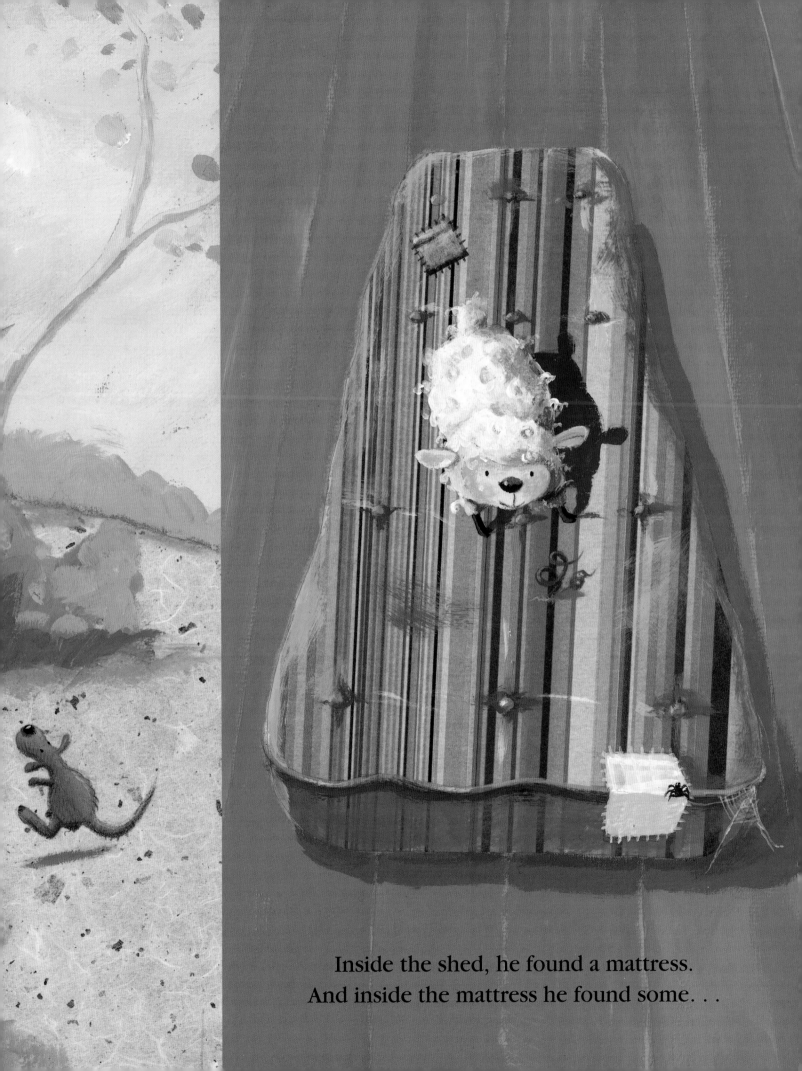

Inside the shed, he found a mattress.
And inside the mattress he found some. . .

springs!

The lamb
had an idea.
He put a spring
on each of his
feet and tried
to jump.

"Hurray!" he yelled. His idea worked.
He could jump really high.

Boing!

He jumped out of the shed.

Boing!

He jumped over the fence.

Boing! Boing! Boing!

He jumped across the yard.

He was so busy jumping that he
didn't notice his maa was watching him.

"Look at me. Look at me!" he shouted.
"I can jump just like you."
His maa hopped out of the
house wearing an old blanket.

"Look at me. Look at me!"
she shouted.
"I'm covered in wool
just like you."

The lamb stopped jumping. He looked at his maa
and felt very sad. He couldn't see her arms.
He couldn't see her brown fur. And worst of all,
he couldn't see her safe, warm pouch.

"You don't look like
my maa anymore," he cried.

"And you don't look like
my lamb," cried his maa.

The lamb looked down
and saw that she was right.
The springs were big and twisty.
They had sharp, pointy ends.
There was no way he could
fit in his maa's pouch with
them on his feet.

The lamb pulled off his springs as quickly as he could!
Then his maa threw away her blanket so they
both looked liked themselves again.

The lamb jumped happily back into his maa's pouch.
For the very first time, he didn't mind being different.
He didn't mind having a thick woolly coat.
He didn't mind not being able to do huge jumps.
He was perfectly happy to be the only

Lamb-a-roo

in the world!